D1455082

Henry's Nap

Illustrated by The Artful Doodlers

Random House New York
Thomas the Tank Engine & Friends™

CREATED BY BRITT ALLCROFT

Based on The Railway Series by The Reverend W Awdry. © 2010 Gullane (Thomas) LLC.
Thomas the Tank Engine & Friends and Thomas & Friends are trademarks of Gullane (Thomas) Limited.
HIT and the HIT Entertainment logo are trademarks of HIT Entertainment Limited.

www.stepintoreading.com   www.randomhouse.com/kids   www.thomasandfriends.com

Educators and librarians, for a variety of teaching tools, visit us at
www.randomhouse.com/teachers

ISBN: 978-0-375-85368-5   MANUFACTURED IN CHINA

HiT entertainment

Henry.

Henry can not go.

He can not get wet.

Henry sits and sits.

Henry can nap.

Tap, tap, tap.

Henry can not nap.

Thomas.

Thomas can go!

He can get wet.

Thomas can go and go.

Henry can not go.

Peep! Peep!
Go, Henry, go!

Thomas and Henry go, go, go.